T0397870

FIRST EXPERIENCES

RYA'S FIRST RECITAL

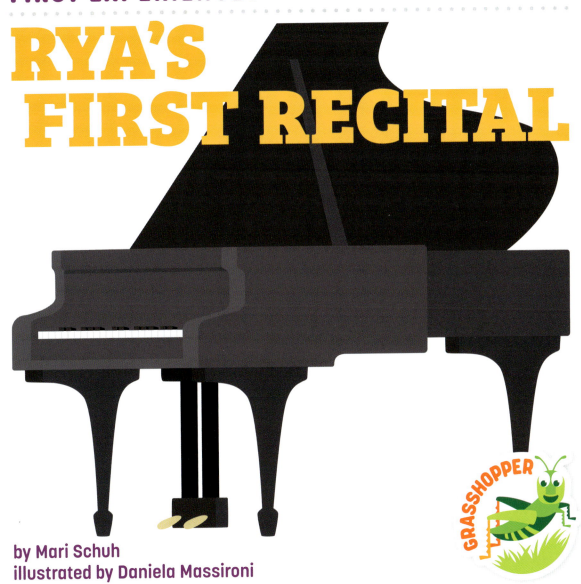

by Mari Schuh
illustrated by Daniela Massironi

Tools for Parents & Teachers

Grasshopper Books enhance imagination and introduce the earliest readers to fiction with fun storylines and illustrations. The easy-to-read text supports early reading experiences with repetitive sentence patterns and sight words.

Before Reading

- Look at the cover illustration. What do readers see? What do they think the book will be about?
- Look at the picture glossary together. Sound out the words. Ask readers to identify the first letter of each vocabulary word.

Read the Book

- "Walk" through the book, reading to or along with the reader. Point to the illustrations as you read.

After Reading

- Review the picture glossary again. Ask readers to locate the words in the text.
- Ask the reader: How does Rya feel before the recital? How does she feel during and after? How do you know?

Grasshopper Books are published by Jump!
5357 Penn Avenue South
Minneapolis, MN 55419
www.jumplibrary.com

Copyright © 2023 Jump! International copyright reserved in all countries. No part of this book may be reproduced in any form without written permission from the publisher.

Library of Congress Cataloging-in-Publication Data

Names: Schuh, Mari C., 1975- author.
Massironi, Daniela, illustrator.
Title: Rya's first recital / by Mari Schuh; illustrated by Daniela Massironi.
Description: Minneapolis, MN: Jump!, Inc., [2023]
Series: First experiences
Audience: Ages 4-7.
Identifiers: LCCN 2021059779 (print)
LCCN 2021059780 (ebook)
ISBN 9781636909332 (hardcover)
ISBN 9781636909349 (paperback)
ISBN 9781636909356 (ebook)
Subjects: LCSH: Readers (Primary)
Concerts–Juvenile fiction.
LCGFT: Readers (Publications)
Classification: LCC PE1119.2 .S3768 2023 (print)
LCC PE1119.2 (ebook)
DDC 428.6/2–dc23/eng/20211217
LC record available at https://lccn.loc.gov/2021059779
LC ebook record available at https://lccn.loc.gov/2021059780

Editor: Jenna Gleisner
Direction and Layout: Anna Peterson
Illustrator: Daniela Massironi

Printed in the United States of America at Corporate Graphics in North Mankato, Minnesota.

Table of Contents

First Time on Stage	4
Let's Review!	16
Picture Glossary	16

First Time on Stage

"I keep messing up! Do I have to play at the recital?" I ask.

The next day is the recital.

I see a lot of people in the audience.

My heart beats fast.

My stomach hurts.

"I don't want everyone to watch me play," I tell my teacher. "What if I mess up?"

"Just take a breath. Then keep playing. It is your turn!" she says.

I walk across the stage.

I see my family!

They smile and wave at me.

I feel better.

I start to play.

Oh, no! I miss a note.

I take a breath.

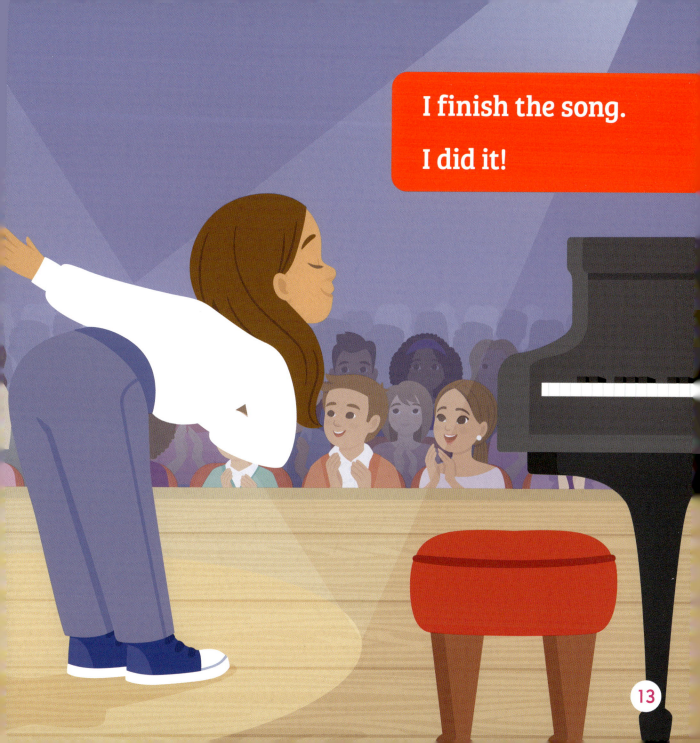

"Great job!" my family says.

"That was fun!" I say. "I am ready for my next recital!"

Let's Review!

Rya is nervous before her recital. How does she know she is nervous?

A. Her heart beats fast. **B.** She smiles.
C. Her stomach hurts. **D.** She feels hungry.

Picture Glossary

audience
The people who watch or listen to a performance.

nervous
Anxious or worried about something.

recital
A performance given by a single person or small group.

stage
A raised platform on which people perform.